# MAX FOUND
# TWO STICKS

To Andrea, who inspires me to hear life's music

—B.P.

# Max Found Two Sticks

## Brian Pinkney

SIMON & SCHUSTER BOOKS FOR YOUNG READERS
Published by Simon & Schuster
New York
London
Toronto
Sydney
Tokyo
Singapore

It was a day when Max didn't feel like talking to anyone. He just sat on his front steps and watched the clouds gather in the sky.

A strong breeze shook the tree in front of his house, and Max saw two heavy twigs fall to the ground.

"What are you gonna do with those sticks?"
Max's grandpa asked as he washed the front
windows.

Not saying a word, Max tapped on his thighs,
*Pat . . . pat-tat.*

*Putter-putter . . . pat-tat.* His rhythm imitated the
sound of the pigeons, startled into flight.

When Max's mother came home carrying new hats for his twin sisters, she asked, "What are you doing with Grandpa's cleaning bucket, Son?"

Max responded by patting the bucket, *Tap-tap-tap*.

*Tippy-tip . . . tat-tat.* He created the rhythm of the light rain falling against the front windows.

After a while the clouds moved on and the sun appeared.
Cindy, Shaun and Jamal showed up drinking sodas.
"Hey, Max! Whatcha doin' with those hatboxes?"

Again Max didn't answer. He just played on the boxes,
*Dum . . . dum-de-dum.*

*Di-di-di-di. Dum-dum.*
Max drummed the beat of the tom-toms in a marching band.

"What are you up to with those soda
bottles?" his dad asked as he brought
out the garbage cans on his way to work.

Max answered on the bottles,
*Dong . . . dang . . . dung.*

*Ding . . . dong . . . ding!* His music joined the chiming of the bells in the church around the corner.

Soon the twins came out to show off their new hats.
"Hey, Max," they asked, "what are you doin' with those
garbage cans?"

Max hammered out a reply on the cans,
*Cling . . . clang . . . da-BANG!*

*A-cling-clang . . . DA-BANGGGG!*
Max pounded out the sound of the wheels thundering
down the tracks under the train on which his
father worked as a conductor.

Suddenly Max heard *Thump-di-di-thump* . . .
*THUMP-DI-DI-THUMP!* as a marching
band rounded the corner.

Max watched the drummers with amazement as they passed,
copying their rhythms. The last drummer saw Max.
Then with a nod and a wink, he tossed Max his spare
set of sticks.

"Thanks," called Max—and he didn't miss a beat.

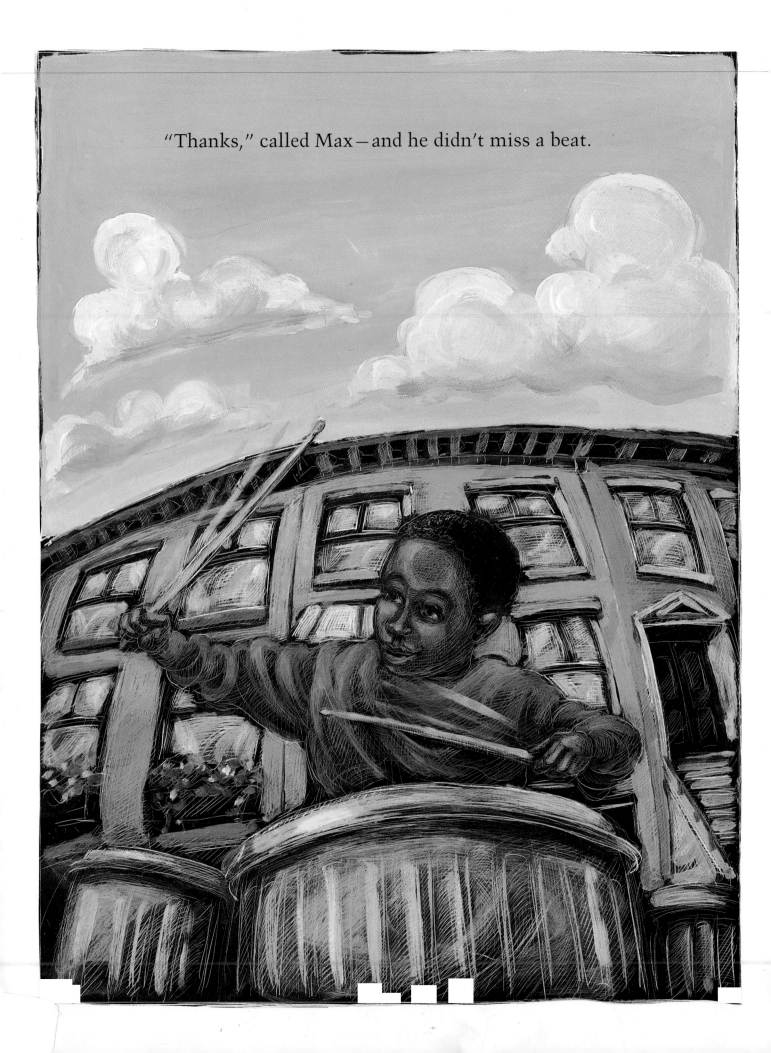

SIMON & SCHUSTER BOOKS FOR YOUNG READERS
Simon & Schuster Building, Rockefeller Center
1230 Avenue of the Americas, New York, New York 10020
Copyright © 1994 by Brian Pinkney.
All rights reserved including the right of reproduction
in whole or in part in any form.
SIMON & SCHUSTER BOOKS FOR YOUNG READERS
is a trademark of Simon & Schuster.
Designed by David Neuhaus.
The text for this book is set in 14 point Trump Mediaeval.
The illustrations were done on scratchboard with oil paint and gouache.
Manufactured in the United States of America

10 9 8 7 6 5 4 3 2

Library of Congress Cataloging-in-Publication Data
Pinkney, J. Brian. Max Found Two Sticks / by Brian Pinkney.
p. cm. Summary: Although he doesn't feel like talking, a young boy
responds to questions by drumming on various objects,
including a bucket, hat boxes, and garbage cans.
[1. Drum—Fiction. 2. Afro-Americans—Fiction.] I. Title
PZ7.P63324Max 1994 [E]—dc20 93-12525 CIP
ISBN: 0-671-78776-4